AF267714

The Journey to Success

KEVIN GO

CONTENTS

Introduction

In this eBook, we will be discussing what success is; what it means to be successful, challenges one will face through the road to success and how to overcome the said challenges.

While success might be a generic answer to what the majority of us are seeking, the perception of success is usually anything but generic. Working in an educational institution, I find it fascinating how diverse success can be interpreted by different individuals. To some, success is purely financial based. While to others, it is defined through their life experiences or ability to contribute back to society, or even having achieved a particular job title. To others, success is measured through their job satisfaction level, work/life balance, or even a combination of those. Regardless of how it is perceived, the important factor in achieving success is to know what it personally means. It should be taken into consideration that an individual's definition of success often changes over time depending on one's life stage and situation.

If you want to achieve something in life you have to work hard for it. If you want to be a basketball player, you have to work hard in school and on the court. Imagine how many people want the same dream as you have, you should then make sure to work harder than the rest. Everyone has an ambition, whether it's towards the positive or negative. Without knowing how one defines success, attaining it will be impossible as they will never know when it is achieved. Ultimately, success is just an overall macro goal and like all goals, if not well defined, the journey becomes similar to one without a compass (or GPS nowadays). It is beneficial to take some time and contemplate what success means to you.

- Re-asses your current path and evaluate if it fits in achieving your *success*.
- If needed, make adjustments to ensure you are on track.
- Press forward while not forgetting to enjoy the journey.

The last point is especially important since it is the journey we take that makes your *success* rewarding. Paying attention and enjoying the journey allows us to appreciate our end goals even more since we're aware of the struggles we have to go through to acquire such. Likewise, we become more aware of our lessons learned, personal growth, and accomplishments. In the end, it is all about understanding what you want out of life and getting out to achieving it while relishing the journey. Now, ask yourself, what does success currently mean to you? Some have ambitions that may lead toward a negative outcome. For example, Macbeth wanted to be king so he killed King Duncan. Macbeth knew that killing King Duncan was not the right thing to do, but he was pressured by his wife. When you have a goal, you will do anything to reach it even if it means stepping out of your comfort zone.

Throughout childhood and early adulthood, we learn various ideas of success from our parents, teachers, and friends. Everyone has their own vision of how and what we should be. It is OK to value the opinion and hopes of others for us. However, we should not adopt them as our own. No one should impose their version of success on us. No one should tell us how it is to live a good life.

It is easy to assume that success means obtaining something concrete or tangible, such as a job title or social status. Nevertheless, do note that some of the greatest success stories resulted from failures. *Success is not final, failure is not fatal.* It is the courage to continue that counts. It is essential to understand that we are successful in many other ways. If we don't acknowledge those little successes when reaching our main goal, we will never be happily satisfied. We have to recognize all our accomplishments.

Ask yourself some questions like:

- Where have I already seen success in my life?
- How can I continue building on that success?
- What lessons have I learned from those successes?
- What have I learned about myself from those areas?

Success is both a goal and a journey. Reaching certain milestones is an element of success. But we don't stop in small milestones; we push higher and harder and strive for more to be better. And before moving forward, you must assess where you are now. This is the time for honest evaluation. Where are you currently successful? Where do you need to grow? What are your weaknesses and strengths? Ask a friend or close colleague to act as your real and unbiased sounding board.

If you do not define your success, someone else will define it for you. What mountain are you climbing? Is it the right one? Or are you going to reach the summit and see your mountain off in the distance?

Every person thinks differently about prosperity in life and defines success in various ways. There is no existing definition that is suitable for all. It is very important that you know exactly how to define your success in life. Make yourself aware of what accomplishment, success, and prosperity means to you in your life. Some might define success as having luxurious cars and a huge mansion, whereas others consider a life full of joy and happiness with their family as the true meaning of success. Once you have figured out what is important to you, then you are able to focus on your visions and goals.

Everything you think about repeatedly will manifest one day. So, think of what you want and you will get what you've asked for. Ask for good things by thinking of good things.

> If you have an appointment with the dentist and you are feeling afraid, picture yourself in this: You're on the dentist chair, imagine great white light enveloping you and say, "Only healing hands touch me". Picture yourself there in the future having a good relaxing time, totally safe in the hands of someone who healed you from the pain.
>
> If you have a job interview, picture yourself in the room. What clothes are you wearing? How is your hair? What perfume do you have on? Imagine yourself filled with confidence. You talk fluently, you are sure of yourself and your talents are obvious.
>
> Are your parents coming to visit? Are you getting exhausted by the idea? Change your mind set! Picture yourself inviting your parents, opening the door, being calm and open-minded, spending a wonderful time with them. See yourself having a conversation with your parents; you keep yourself in their presence. You feel how you love them and you feel their love for you.

Try these and see what happens! It is all in the mind!

Meaning of Success

We cannot define success without knowing what failure is. The opposite of success is failure. You may fail while trying to achieve your objectives. Wealthy and successful people also fail in their lives. Just think about the rich and famous and all their scandals, addictions and suicides. All of them were extraordinary people but a lot of them were also extremely unhappy with their lives and were not able to grasp the true meaning of success. Wealth cannot be defined with money alone. It is defined by the small things that make you a happy person, such as, friendship, family, inner peace and more.

Now, we can define success as the status of having accomplished an objective. Being successful means achieving the desired vision and planned goals. Furthermore, success can be a social status that describes a prosperous person that has gained fame for its favorable outcome. The dictionary describes *success* as: attaining wealth, prosperity and/ or fame.

One of the most important steps to achieve success in life is to know your personal life's meaning of success. The true meaning of success goes far beyond the common definitions of success, which are: being wealthy, having a lot of material things and earned educational degrees. Quite the opposite, true success in life cannot be measured with the above-mentioned, but instead, with the number of people that are able to live a better life because of what you've created. This is the meaning of success. It is not the trophies people collect in their lives. Media and society often make us conclude that living a successful life means to be extraordinarily wealthy with material things. The meaning of success is to live a happy life and to make this world a better place for everyone.

WHAT IS THE DIFFERENCE BETWEEN ACCOMPLISHMENT AND SUCCESS?

Accomplishment is often associated with success, but it's not the same. Accomplishment refers to the results we desire when attempting to reach certain goals. Basically, it's the outcome that we plan or desire to happen. Success is the positive consequence or product of an accomplishment. Accomplishment can be seen as the process to become successful and with every accomplished goal, you take a step towards prosperity and a life full of success.

WHAT IT MEANS TO BE SUCCESSFUL

All of us want to succeed in life. We want to accomplish something, to feel in some way that we have "won". It is easy to get sucked into thinking that we have to succeed through the world's generic perception of it, when really; we each need to define success for ourselves.

WHY SUCCESS IS NOT MONEY

We all know that money does not always make us happy. Beyond a certain level of security, having more money would not make a difference. You can always buy another gadget or splurge out on a better bottle of wine, but will a few extra megapixels on your camera really matter? Would you even notice the difference between a $10 and a $100 bottle of wine? A big bank balance might be nice to look at, but it can never replace the love of family and friends or the sense of fulfilment gained by doing work that you enjoy. You could be earning $100,000, working through 60-hours a week in a job that you hate. Does that imply success? I would have to say, no, it does not.

SUCCESS IS NOT ABOUT HAVING STUFF

Sometimes, we treat success as if it is a game where we need to rack up as many points as possible. We think success means having a particular career, or owning a lot of flashy gadgets. Your family, properties and career do matter. But with these alone, are they considered a "success"? Is your unmarried uncle a failure because he chose to travel the world and work for charities, rather than buying a house, settling down and having a family? I would say, no, he is not.

SUCCESS IS LIVING YOUR BEST LIFE

So what exactly is success? Well, there is no single definition. Success is about living your best life, and only you can say what that means. It does not matter what your friends or parents or the society thinks. Defining success is up to you. Perhaps, to you, success means having enough money to get by and having as much free time as possible. It might mean getting recognition in a particular field, maybe as an artist or a musician. For some people, success might be about raising happy, healthy children.

In my opinion, success is getting yourself the kind of life you want. This should be the kind of life you whole- heartedly want, one that will make you happy. For others, success will be defined differently since various things make different people happy. For me, happiness is having a happy family that gets to spend time together. We may have achieved success through education; having good education to get a stable job and through some sacrifice, like: 'no longer working full-time so I can stay home with the kids'. Success definitely varies for different people.

I believe success is in the point of your life where you feel content with what you have and what you have achieved. Success can be achieved at any age, though many people may not feel they have already succeeded in life. In society, money is considered by many to be the measure of success. If that is the case, then why do wealthy people fall into drugs, alcohol or other destructive behaviors? I believe to achieve success you need to have goals in life. Work hard and the rest will fall into place.

Success is a completely relative term. Gandhi was incredibly successful in my opinion and he owned only three sets of clothes. Bill Gates is also successful and he's worth over $50 billion. So the question becomes: what do you want to achieve in your lifetime, how do you want to live your life? You cannot say that a man is successful if he is rich. Success is attained by your own satisfaction, and it is funny how you won't know that you have succeeded until someone points it out to you. To succeed in life, you have to find your own field of interest and work 'smart' towards it. Success can be defined in different ways for different people.

STAGES OF SUCCESS

GOAL

You have created something of so much value to everyone that the value gets reflected back to you, like a reflection in a pond on a clear day. People look up to you. Money continuously comes in. This may feel like success. But, so many people might get pleasure from this that your "success" knows no bounds. So this definition might be suspect.

HAPPY

You are happy with a spouse, job, place, and your private creative achievements. You wake up and the birds sing. You are happy. But we all know we age and people die. Creativity always carries on its back the weight of the criticisms all too eager to pile on. This success is fleeting hence suspect.

HEALTHY

I always advocate for a daily practice. Every day, attempt to improve at least 1% of your physical, emotional, mental, and spiritual pillars.

This has been the only thing that has worked for me when I am at my lowest points.

FREEDOM

Some of us are in man-made prisons, forced to do what we do not want to do to feed our families and stay alive. Some of us are in self-imposed prisons, "if I do not do THIS then I have FAILED."

The best way to have a successful tomorrow, a successful life, and a successful legacy, is to have a successful moment NOW.

For me being successful could be:

- When your parents are overwhelmed with happiness that their eyes are filled with tears.
- When a stranger on the road knows about your achievement and waits for you alone in the street hoping for your return from work to get your advice.
- When the friends who never looked you up in the past suddenly turn up to becoming like your best friends.
- When someone fights to be a part of your success for the sake of their own fame.
- When you get tired thanking everyone who wished you well for your success.
- When your family treats you with great respect as if you achieved the world.
- When you realize a lot of people know you through the number of likes/comments you get on social media.
- When someone asks for your personal advice on their life and their goals.
- When someone looks up to you as their role model.
- When someone, who is not your blood relative but is in some way related to you, feels proud of your achievement.

- When a hater asks you how you've achieved your goal.
- When you do not realize what great of an impact you have done after seeing all the changes around you.
- When you realize that this is not the end of it all and you have so much more to achieve in life.

Ways to Make One Successful

Let's be honest, success is hard. Not complicated, just hard. I want to rewire how you think about success and teach you how to be successful in life. People tend to have a misconstrued definition of success. We love to say things like:

> *"I will be successful once I find a career related to my passion."*

> *"I will be a success when I make my first million dollars."*

> *"I will be a success when I find the love of my life."*

The truth is success is not a goal or a destination; it is a MINDSET you take on to achieve your goals. And like all other mindsets, you do not just drop it once you achieve your goals. Instead, you inculcate it unto yourself so you can carry it with you forever.

Below are ways you can be successful:

FOCUS ON COMMITMENT, NOT MOTIVATION.

Just how committed are you to your goal? How important is it for you, and what are you willing to sacrifice in order to achieve it? If you find yourself fully committed, motivation will follow.

SEEK KNOWLEDGE, NOT RESULTS.

If you focus on the excitement of discovery, improvement, exploration and experimenting, your motivation will always be fuelled. If you focus only on results, your motivational fire will depreciate. So the key is to focus on the journey, not the destination. Keep thinking about what you are learning along the way and what you can improve.

MAKE THE JOURNEY FUN.

It is an awesome experience! The minute you take it in too seriously, there is a chance it will start weighing you down emotionally and you will lose perspective and be stuck again.

GET RID OF STAGNATING THOUGHTS.

Thoughts influence feelings and feelings determine how you view your work. You have a lot of thoughts in your head, and you always have a choice of which ones to focus on: the ones that will keep you stuck (fears, doubts) or the ones that will push you forward (excitement, experimenting, exploration).

USE YOUR IMAGINATION.

After getting rid of negative thoughts, use your imagination. When things go well, you are full of positive energy and when you are experiencing difficulties, you need to be even more energetic. So, rename your situation. If you keep repeating, *"I hate my work."* guess what feeling will it evoke? It is a matter of imagination! You can always find something to learn even from the worst boss in the world at the most boring job. I have a good exercise for you: For three days, think and say positive things. See what happens.

STOP BEING NICE TO YOURSELF.

Motivation means action and action brings results. Sometimes your actions fail to bring the results you want. So you prefer to be nice and not put pressure to yourself. You wait for the perfect timing, for an opportunity, while you drive yourself into stagnation and sometimes even into depression. Get out there! Challenge yourself! Be courageous and do something you want even when you are afraid.

GET RID OF DISTRACTIONS.

Distractions and worthless things will always get in your way. Avoid any band aid solutions. Get out of your comfort zone and find other ways to be more efficient in accomplishing your tasks. Learn to redirect your focus on your priorities rather than dwelling on the insignificant. Write a list of time-wasters and hold yourself off from doing these.

DO NOT RELY ON OTHERS.

You should never expect others to do things for you; not even your partner, your best friend or boss. They too are busy with their own needs. No one will make you happy nor achieve your goals for you. It has to be all done by YOU.

PLAN.

Know your three-steps forward. Fill out your weekly calendar, noting when you will do what and how. When-what-how is important in scheduling. Also, at the end of the day, review how each day went, know what you've learned and point out what you could improve.

PROTECT YOURSELF FROM BURNOUT.

It is easy to get burned out when you are very motivated. Observe yourself and acknowledge any signs of fatigue and find time to rest. Give your body and mind rest by including a recreational activity in your schedule. Switch between creative and logical works. Do diverse tasks: do something physical, do work alone, then with a team, change work locations, meditate, or just take deep breaths. Lacking motivation does not mean you are being lazy or being unambitious. Even the biggest stars, richest business people or the most accomplished athletes get lost sometimes. What keeps them driven is the curiosity of how much better or faster they can get. Thus, be curious, and this will get you to your ambitions!

Regardless of your age, status, or what your career goals are, it is likely that your ultimate goal in life is to be happy and successful. Be successful with more than just being wealthy and making a mark, follow your passions, live purposefully, and enjoy the present moment.

IDENTIFY YOUR PASSIONS.

As mentioned earlier, you have to define what success means to you. While it may take years to realize what you want to do with your life, identifying your passions, interests, and values will help you set goals and give your life a sense of meaning. If you have trouble identifying these things, ask a friend or family member to help you. Ask yourself these questions:

- What legacy do you want to leave?
- How would you like to be remembered?
- How can you make your community a better place?
- What are your interests in life? For example, think of the subjects you enjoyed studying in school and ask why you liked them.
- Let's say you're into musical theatre. Ask: Do you like it because you love the music or because you love working with a big group with a common goal?

MAKE A LIST OF YOUR GOALS AND WHAT YOU NEED TO DO TO ACHIEVE THEM.

Be sure to address both short-term and long-term goals. Go beyond financial and career goals. Think about relationship goals, goals for improving yourself, things you would like to learn and experience first-hand. Draw a timeline that indicates when you should achieve each. Have prerequisites for big goals. For example, if your goal is to see the world, then prioritize in saving money first then visit one country at a time.

LIVE PURPOSEFULLY.

In order to achieve your dreams and to be the person you want to be, you have to start paying attention to your actions. Ask yourself, "Are my current actions leading me to where I want to be?" If you're constantly bored and daydreaming about the future or past, or finding yourself counting the minutes until the day ends, these are probably because you are feeling disconnected from what you are doing.

Enjoy your time by doing things that you are fond of while prioritizing your prerequisite tasks. Don't procrastinate. Instead of watching television during the weekends, spend your time doing your hobbies or enjoy your time with loved ones and new friends. Measure your productivity by how much you have engaged yourself in the process and not its output. Your productivity does not have to be done based on a standard definition of a 'finished' task. Your activities should also be fun and engaging.

Keep in mind that it is perfectly fine to take a break and do nothing for a day, doing this can actually stimulate your imagination and self-awareness. Strive for a balance between doing things you want to do and allowing yourself to just "be."

STICK TO YOUR COMMITMENTS.

Planning is not sufficient; keeping your word is more important. If you tell someone you will do something, do it. Similarly, do not tell someone you will do something if you are not sure you can. Be honest about your limits. Avoid cancelling plans. And try not to cancel twice on the same person. Make commitments to yourself, and stick to it. Write these down and hang them in places that you can see.

Make sure that your commitments are gradually moving you towards your goals. Review your goals now and then to make sure you are moving in the right direction. Be educated. Education gives you the knowledge, skills, and credibility to achieve your maximum potential. In terms of financial success, statistics have shown that the more education you have (i.e. the higher degree you achieve), the more money you are likely to make. In 2011, the median weekly earnings for high school graduates were $638 while those with bachelor's degrees made $1053. That same year, those with masters or doctoral degrees made $1263 and $1551 respectively.

Not all education has to be formal. Apprenticeships and long-term training programs are also positively correlated with higher incomes. Obtaining a Certificate in your field can help to increase your salary. Educate yourself for pleasure as well. The more you know about the world you live in, the more questions you will have and the more interested you will be.

MANAGE YOUR FINANCES.

Learning how to manage your money will help ensure your financial stability over time, regardless of your income. Keep track of your expenses. Subtract your monthly expenses from your monthly income to determine how much spending money you have available each month. Also, review your bank statements often and notice where you spend your money. This will help you prevent over-spending and ensure that your bank statements are correct. Understand your income. When calculating your income, be sure to take into account the federal, state, and social security taxes that will be deducted from your gross pay. Do not overlook miscellaneous deductions, such as health insurance premiums, savings bonds, and loan payments. The resulting number is your net pay, which is what you end up taking home with you.

CUT BACK.

If you are not earning enough money to cover your net expenses, then look into your expenses to see where you might be able to cut back.

SAVE MONEY.

Every month, you should deposit some of your money into a savings account. Consider asking your employer to directly deposit a portion of your income into your savings account.

INVEST CAUTIOUSLY.

If your workplace offers a retirement savings plan, put your excess incomes in that.

MANAGE YOUR TIME.

Putting off important tasks until the last minute can cause you unnecessary stress, and increase the likelihood of errors and negligence. Manage your time so that you have enough time to complete tasks effectively. Use a planner to help keep you organized throughout the day, week, and month. Set reminders on your smartphone and make use of its electronic timer for better time management. Make a list of all the things you need to do in a given day, and check off each task as you complete it. This will help you stay organized and motivated.

ENJOY THE PRESENT MOMENT.

If you are constantly dwelling on the past or daydreaming about the future, you are missing out on the present moment. Remember that the past and the future are simply illusions and that real life takes place here and now. Start paying attention to negative thoughts so that you can move on from them and enjoy the present moment. If a negative thought arises in your head, then acknowledge it, label it a negative thought, and then let it fade away. Regular meditation or mindfulness exercises can help to make this feel more natural for you. Get in the habit of paying attention to small details around you. Appreciate the feeling of the sun on your skin, the sensation of your feet walking on the ground, or the artwork in the restaurant you are eating in. Noticing things like these will help you silence a rambling mind and appreciate every moment.

DO NOT COMPARE YOUR OWN LIFE TO OTHER PEOPLES' LIVES.

Unfortunately, many people measure their own success by comparing it to the success of those around them. If you want to feel accomplished and happy, you will have to value your life for its own sake. Many people have the tendency to compare the low points of their own lives with the high points of other peoples' lives. Remember that no matter how perfect somebody's life may seem, behind closed doors everybody deals with tragedy, insecurity, and other difficulties. Pay attention to and limit your use of social media to help you remember this.

Rather than comparing yourself with people who are "better off" than you, think about all of the people who are homeless, chronically ill, or living in poverty. This will help you appreciate what you have rather than feeling sorry for yourself. Try engaging in volunteer work to help make this more apparent. This can help to boost your happiness and confidence as well.

COUNT YOUR BLESSINGS.

No matter how much you achieve in life, you will always feel unhappy if you constantly focus on what you do not have. Instead, devote time every day to appreciating the things you do have. Think beyond material items; appreciate your loved ones, and cherish happy memories.

LOOK AFTER YOUR HEALTH.

A healthy body supports a healthy mind. Eat a balanced diet and ensure that you aren't lacking in any necessary nutrients. Establish the cause of any problems you may experience, such as a lack of energy or a lack of concentration and deal with them by discussing with a doctor, nutritionist, and related health professionals. Get plenty of exercises too but make your fitness choices according to what you enjoy.

FOLLOW UP ON OPPORTUNITIES.

If you have a chance to shine, take it. If you are worried you would not have time and energy for a good opportunity, ask yourself, would this contribute to my end goals? If it would, then get rid of other commitments in order to pursue this opportunity. Remember, some chances only come around once. You cannot bank them. This does not mean you should throw away all your savings or get rid of your safety net. It just means you should say yes when you are given an offer to move ahead.

SURROUND YOURSELF WITH POSITIVE PEOPLE.

Make friends with people you admire for various reasons: because they are happy, kind, generous, successful at work, or successful in other ways. Join forces with those who have achieved things you want to achieve, or who are on their way to a common goal. Do not let jealousy get in your way, nobody's success is a threat to yours. When making friends with someone, ask yourself if the person makes you feel motivated, positive, and confident, or if they make you feel tired, overwhelmed, or incompetent. Choose to spend time with the positive people, not the ones sucking your energy.

If you have friends or family members who always make you feel bad about yourself, limit the time you spend with them. Also, make sure to identify relationships that are not helping you to move towards your goals, that stress you out, or that require too much of your time and energy without being reciprocal. Look for mentors among the people you admire. If you think you could learn from someone, ask for their advice.

SET BOUNDARIES WITH OTHERS.

Advocate for your own needs. Be caring towards others, but do not accept abuse from anyone. Remember, being a good person does not mean you have to take violent or disrespectful language or actions from anyone. Respect the boundaries others set for you, too. Listen to your loved ones when they tell you they need space or want to do something alone. It is fairly easy to be modestly successful; you just have to work hard. It is harder to be very successful; you have to work hard, and smart, and catch a few breaks along the way.

It is extremely difficult to be incredibly successful... yet we all hope to achieve exceptional success.

The key is to bring together a number of traits and qualities, learning to excel or at the very least be outstanding at each. Sound impossible? It is not. And that is why I have collected a number of my most popular posts on how to be successful into one post full of tips and links to helpful, practical advice.

DEVELOP REMARKABLE WILLPOWER AND DETERMINATION.

One way is to see your life and future as totally within your control. There is a quote often credited to Ignatius: "Pray as if God will take care of all; act as if all is up to you." The same premise applies to luck. Many people feel luck has a lot to do with success or failure. If they succeed, luck favored them, and if they fail, luck was against them. Most successful people do feel good luck played some role in their success. But they do not wait for good luck or worry about bad luck. They act as if success or failure is totally within their control. If they succeed, they think they caused it. If they fail, they think they caused it.

By not wasting mental energy worrying about what might happen to you, you can put all your effort into making things happen. You cannot control luck, but you can definitely control you. A lot more on developing remarkable willpower and determination.

MAKE A REMARKABLE FIRST IMPRESSION.

One way is to never try to take before you give.

TAKE NETWORKING.

The goal of networking is to connect with people who can help you make a sale, get a referral, establish a contact, etc. When we network, we want something. Still, at first, do not ask for what you want. Forget about what you can get and focus on what you can provide because giving is the only way to establish a real connection and relationship. Focus solely on what you can get out of the connection and you will never make meaningful, mutually beneficial connections. When you network, it should be all about them, not you. A lot more on making a remarkable first impression.

USE YOUR BODY LANGUAGE TO YOUR ADVANTAGE.

One way is to smile because smiling reduces your stress levels. Frowning, grimacing, and other negative facial expressions signal your brain that whatever you are doing is difficult. So your body responds by releasing cortisol, which raises your stress levels. Stress begets more stress, begets more stress and in no time, you are a hot mess. Here is the cure, Make yourself smile. You'll feel less stress even if nothing else about the situation changes. And there is a bonus when you smile, other people feel less stress, too. Which, of course, will reduce your stress levels? So kill two stresses with one smile.

(By the way, smiling also makes working out easier. Say you are doing reps with a heavyweight; naturally you will grimace. But if you force yourself to smile, you will often find you can do one or two more reps. Try it but be prepared for when other gym rats look at you oddly). A lot more on using body language to your advantage.

BE REMARKABLY AND GENUINELY GIVING.

One way is to give the gift of patience. For some people, we are willing to give our all. Why? They care about us, they believe in us, and we do not want to let them down. Showing patience is an extraordinary way to let people know we truly care about them. Showing patience and expressing genuine confidence is an extraordinary way to let people know we truly believe in them. Showing patience is a remarkable gift because, ultimately, it shows how much you care. A lot more on how to become remarkably giving.

BECOME REMARKABLY EFFECTIVE.

One way is to use your goals to make decisions automatic. In a podcast, Tim Ferriss described how Herb Kelleher, the CEO of Southwest Airlines, makes so many decisions every day. Kelleher applies a simple framework to every issue; will this help southwest be the low-cost provider? If so, the answer is yes. If not, no. Remarkably effective people apply the same framework to the decisions they make. "Will this help me reach my goal? If not, I would not do it." If you feel like you are constantly struggling to make decisions, take a step back. Think about your goals; your goals will help you make decisions.

That is why remarkably effective people are so decisive. Indecision is born of a lack of purpose: When you know what you truly want, most of your decisions can and should be almost automatic. A lot more on becoming remarkably effective.

BECOME REMARKABLY LIKABLE.

One way is to shine the spotlight on others. No one receives enough praise. No one. Be the first to tell people what they did well. Not only will people appreciate your praise, but they will also appreciate the fact you care enough to pay attention to what they are doing. Then they will feel a little more accomplished and a lot more important.

BECOME A REMARKABLE BOSS.

One way is to help your employees find and embrace a true sense of purpose. Everyone likes to feel a part of something bigger. Everyone loves to feel that sense of teamwork and esprit de corps that turn a group of individuals into a real team. The best missions involve making a real impact on the lives of the customers you serve. Let employees know what you want to achieve for your business, for your customers, and even your community. And if you can, let them create a few missions of their own.

Feeling a true purpose starts with knowing what to care about and, more important, why to care.

EMBRACE THE RIGHT MINDSET.

One way is to realize that the people around you are the people you chose. Think about it. Some of your employees drive you nuts. Some of your customers are obnoxious. Some of your friends are selfish, all-about-me jerks. Then think about this, you chose them. If the people around you make you unhappy it is not their fault. It is your fault. They are in your professional or personal life because you drew them to you and you let them remain. Think about the type of people you want to work with. Think about the types of customers you would enjoy serving. Think about the friends you want to have.

Then change what you do so you can start attracting those people. Hardworking people want to work with hardworking people. Kind people like to associate with kind people. Remarkable employees want to work for remarkable bosses. Successful people are naturally drawn to successful people.

SEE BEING HAPPY AS A CHOICE YOU GET TO MAKE, BECAUSE IT IS.

One way is to make money, but also make memories. Sure, money is important. Money does a lot of things. (One of the most crucial being that it creates options.) But beyond a certain point, money does not make people happier. After about $75,000 a year, money does not buy more (or less) happiness. "Beyond $75,000... higher income is neither the road to experience happiness nor the road to the relief of unhappiness or stress," say the authors of one study.

They go on to say: "Perhaps $75,000 is the threshold beyond which further increases in income no longer improve individuals' ability to do what matters most to their emotional well-being, such as spending time with people they like, avoiding pain and disease, and enjoying leisure." And if you do not buy that, here is another take: "The materialistic drive and satisfaction with life are negatively related." Or, in layman's terms, "Chasing possessions tends to make you less happy." Think of it as the bigger house syndrome. You want a bigger house. You need a bigger house. So you buy it. Life is good. Until a couple of months later when your bigger house is now just your house.

NEW ALWAYS BECOMES THE NEW NORMAL.

"Things" provide only momentary bursts of happiness. To be happier, do not chase as many things. Chase a few experiences instead.

Challenges One Would Face On the Road to Success

FEAR

If we need to succeed, we have to believe challenges are likely to happen and be ready to confront challenges. That is challenging our challenges. And this confrontation should be made in line with achieving our plans in our life. However, some persons understand that confronting challenges in our road to success are results of ill-planned tasks and such persons confronting are reckless and irresponsible. And this is a hasty generalization. It is wise and mandatory to face and confront challenges to reach our best destiny.

Actually, confronting challenges should be waged according to our personal abilities, experiences, and opportunities since trying to confront devastating challenges might take us out of the game. So, everyone is expected to wage confrontations in the extent of his personal life abilities, experiences and situations in determination and hope to be a man/woman of success. Sitting idle and feared to confront problems might be relieved from committing mistakes, but failing to confront challenges is better than failing without confronting challenges.

Therefore, to be a successful person in our life, it is natural to pass through challenges. Hence we have to be self-confident, meticulous and decision maker to our own lives as well as we have to be a marksman/woman in defeating problems posing challenging burdens to our success.

LACK OF PERSISTENT DETERMINATION

When we perceive that problems are unavoidable and unchallenging, we prefer to give up our confrontation. This is our everyday factual scenario in our marriage/spousal and personal relationships. This opposes to characters of successful/victorious persons. It is an open truth and fact that victorious persons sustain interim failures, but not surrendered to failures believing their failure in advance. Being failed for some time does not mean that we remain failed forever. Here I am not advocating lodging persistent struggle in any trivial and insignificant matters but on fruitful and tasks resulting in positive changes. As such we need to struggle with our problems in determination conceiving hope for a bright future.

THE DESIRE TO SUCCEED OVERNIGHT

Every person's desire to be a millionaire brings and expands the lottery business. It is becoming a common practice see persons depressed caused by contemplating multifarious ideas overnight to meet their success within a short period of time. To be free from such problem most persons take sleeping pills at night. Really, it is a joy to succeed without going too long, however, in marching to shortcut paths we are not aware of and ready to face devastating challenges. Desiring to succeed overnight leads to develop a limited vision in life. Developing limited vision prohibits could not bring sustainable objectives benefiting you long in your life. That is persons who have limited visions are not far-sighted, progressive and a difference maker. They are persons of a day even who could not bring lasting solutions.

CUTTING CORNERS

In conjunction with the above, most persons who desire to succeed overnight look for shortcuts without calculating difficulties on each and every walks on shortcuts. They simply draw in bringing the already desired achievement to the ground in a shortcut, in short-range. Actually, such type of persons might succeed for the time being, but their end is failure and impoverishment/destitution. For this, persons who are engaged in prostitution and contraband trade and students known for their cheating behavior are good examples.

FAILURE TO PUT FIRST THINGS FIRST

Usually, persons are observed in accomplishing tomorrow tasks leaving today's prior activities. For example in affection, a person who is in love is seen forwarding valuable gifts and money before showing and forwarding his/her innermost passion or love for his friend. Failure to give priority for basic our tasks wastes our effort and time. And a wasted effort and time result in a wasted/ fruitless life. Please put first things first.

SELFISHNESS AND GREEDINESS

Persons and organizations known for their selfish and greedy behavior should not bother about societal change and development. Because they can do anything at the expense of others for themselves. Selfishness and greediness have no any destination they can achieve their goal. The always march everlastingly. These two are evil/malicious acts of some human behavior, especially those who are corrupt. They resulted from the habit of falsifying, bombastic behavior and the habit of giving less value to oneself. To avoid them, we have to develop a culture of living by ourselves being dependent on ourselves. But, leaving selfish and greedy behavior does not mean that we have to sit idle lacking the courage and effort to improve ourselves. Selfishness and greediness oust human beings from the cage of humanity and destines to bad ends. For instance, a corrupted person either imprisoned or become a capitally punished and killed.

SUBMISSIVENESS

Persons deprived of self-confidence in their stand and ideas remain in at the mid-way and defeated by back runners. Submissive persons do not have a self-confidence on their acts and beliefs. They simply follow other's stand even if they aware not on the right path, or others they are following are mistaken. This supporting the malicious or mistaken act or the idea of persons visibly. To be a successful person, you have to be a supporter of your idea and act. You have to be part of a solution to the problem. Weak stand erodes your strong belief. Strong belief causes miraculous achievements, do not wait till miraculous things happen. If you have not a strong belief you are not yourself. You are a person of others and a person of failure and defeat in lifespan.

FAILURE TO UNDERSTAND NATURAL LAWS

It is always said that there is no novel thing below the sun. This means all achievements and transformations of life is based upon and within nature. Unless you know the law of nature, you cannot be successful in your life. So, success is the mystery of understanding and practicing natural laws. Change is an aspect of natural law. Everlastingly, there is a change in the lives of human beings. Either we move back or forth, it is changing. However, every change is not a success. Only a change reasonably acceptable to us important is a success. A change which is not reasonable is disastrous to us. This means in our endeavor to change, we have to be reasonable. Is it for good or bad? If it is for bad, it is not a reasonable change that leads to success. So, we have to understand that our changes are successes when it goes in line with nature.

DO NOT WANT TO PLAN AND BE READY/ PREPARED

Most persons are seen planning to use their time on recreational activities and parties than their futurity. Self-confidence only develops from planning our destiny and the readiness to practice accordingly. Readiness means avoiding acceptance of failure, but it entertains failure and learns from mistakes or experiences of defeat or failure. Our success depends upon our readiness and the burden we swear to carry out plans. As such victorious persons are seen shouldering burdensome tasks. Thereby, their self-confidence grows in the extent they accept burdensome activities to accomplish. So we can become successful when we become so ready to accomplish plans skillful and ethical manner. For this, we have to be committed to paying sacrifice to bring success to the limelight of our life.

ENLISTING TRIVIAL REASONS OR PRETEXTS

Enlisting multitude of reasons for failure or defeat and making pretexts is not the habit of successful persons. When unsuccessful persons asked reasons for their failure, they list several of them. Among those, the following can be mentioned:

- I am not lucky;
- I am not created for success;
- I am disabled;
- I am not wise;

- I am not educated;
- I am not so pretty or handsome;
- I am not in close contact with persons;
- I do not have enough money;
- The country's situation is not permitting;
- I have not met the opportunities;
- I do not have a family;
- I do not have a supportive staff or partner. And so on.

To list such pretexts and to compromise our defeat; nothing can be created. Actually, such aforementioned reasons create inconvenience, but they couldn't harness us not to succeed if we have the courage, determination to pass through challenges. They cannot bring any positive prospective effect; rather they take us back to another failure.

FAILURE TO LEARN FROM PAST MISTAKES

Failures and past mistakes are not ends by themselves; rather they are learning tools to our futurity. We should not recurrently curse our past mistakes and attribute trivial reasons and make fruitful pretexts, rather we have to learn from failures not to repeat again another time. Mistakes are our future devising tools to escape likely challenges. There is no person who cannot make a mistake. But, he or she who does the same mistake is a fool. So, the secret of success is taking experience from past mistakes.

FAILURE TO CONSIDER/STUDY OPPORTUNITIES

Life-changing and improving opportunities are existent when challenges face us. God-sent opportunities are not only found made to a lottery winner, but also for the one who faced challenges. Challenges happen for good. For example, if challenges have not tested us, when and how we know our strength and ability? So, if challenges assist us as such, they are opportunities for success. Do not fear challenges, but ready to face and thereby defeat.

FAILURE TO USE OUR TALENT

Than regretting when we aged and reach the verge of death, it is marvelous to use our talent. Mostly, it is said that he is only Albert Einstein who used his one-fourth talent. So, others passed away with their talent. Everyone is born with her/his own talent. And we should have to believe that we have an immense talent. Thereby it is required to endeavor persistently with courage, determination, hope and in patience.

LACK OF DISCIPLINE

Why some persons suffer failures in trading, education, farming and so on? And why do some others become successful? It is because of discipline matters. Discipline is a tool to enhance our commitment, responsibility, self-management, positive thinking and is a tool to avoid mistakes. Failure to be disciplined bears mistake and unforgettable regret. Be disciplined is for oneself, not for others. It is for the sake of our success.

GIVING LITTLE PLACE FOR ONESELF (LOOKING DOWN ONESELF)

This sort of obstacle to our success results from not paying due attention and respect for oneself as a human being. If you do not give a place/respect to yourself, you cannot even become a leader of yourself. Persons who do not respect themselves are on the way to identify and know themselves. Such types of persons are those who have an identity crisis. To be relieved from such a crisis, you have to believe that you are fully a human person who can do anything amazing/ successful like other persons.

LACK OF KNOWLEDGE

If a person learns and becomes acquiring a better knowledge, he or she will able to understand areas he or she lacks the required knowledge. If you believe that I am knowledge, you are expected to learn so far. This is not to look down yourself, but to benefit in adding knowledge that shines your life in the future ahead. In your every day to day activity, you have to develop the curiosity to know novel things better.

BAD PERCEPTION/LACK OF POSITIVE THINKING

Developing bad perception takes you back and success goes too far from you. Persons who lack positive thinking do not believe in an effort to succeed, rather they attribute the key to success with luck and wizardly. Such type of persons engages in their work half-heartedly. They do not know their ability and talent. Their identity is swallowed by their bad perception conceived. If you need to succeed in your life, first and foremost avoid such bad perceptions.

LACK OF AIM/OBJECTIVE

For each and every activity you are carrying out, you have to be reasonable taking into account your formerly stated objectives. Aim or objective means a strong and heartedly conceived desire at your heart and mind you need to succeed. Persons, who lack their own aim or objective, do not know where to go, they do not have any courage, discipline or ethics, and they are aimless shooters.

LACK OF COURAGE

Successful persons do not expect miracles, shortcuts, or do not see others' harassing and discouraging act; but they need to look for ways to pass through challenges. They see how much remains to go but do not count how much they went, they conceived hope with determination, effort, and patience for success. Prayers to success only become effective when you accomplish your tasks with courage. Courage and discipline are prime spices to success, and they are differentiating factors between ordinary and successful persons. Courage illuminates our fear, it defeats fear. Let us develop courage in our efforts to succeed.

How to Overcome Challenges on Your Journey to Success

Life is full of challenges. Some people seem to meet every challenge with confidence, while others struggle to overcome them. Pittas especially get a sense of satisfaction from facing challenges head-on; it brings a sense of accomplishment and can be very fulfilling. On some level, you actually seek challenges. Your highest self wants you to learn and grow, and life's most effective tool toward growth is the experience. The problem is that all too often you might find yourself faced with the same challenges over and over again, and that's when you start to lose motivation to face the issue and you lose sight of the potential lesson. At that point, challenges can become problems that can spiral you into despair and frustration.

As a co-creator of your own reality, you have the ability to overcome these challenges. It is with this sense of responsibility and awareness that you can begin your journey into a higher state of consciousness where challenges are no longer challenges, but opportunities to get a glimpse of your highest self.

Here are some ways to better accept and meet your personal challenges, whatever they may be.

FACE THE CHALLENGE

In many cases, this is the most important step, the most obvious step, yet it is also the most often missed. People spend time looking for a way around the issue, or wallowing in despair at the enormity of the challenge, instead of facing it. Even mundane things, like a pileup of laundry or work, get ignored. Putting a challenge off does not make it go away. This is true of big challenges, as well as the small ones. The most important thing you can do is face what's in front of you, head on.

BE PRESENT

Do not underestimate the power of being present. If you make a practice of facing your challenges even in failure with full presence and awareness, you will find most challenges are not challenges at all. Instead, life's challenges become messages from the universe. Meditation can help you cultivate silent awareness and is a good tool to help bring that focus to yourself during difficult times. You can ask yourself questions that help you better understand the problem and how it affects you.

- Why is this a challenge?
- Do I believe that I am capable of being successful in this challenge?
- What are the possible outcomes if I succeed?
- What is the outcome if I fail?

These questions are not meant to solve the problem, rather they are meant to help bring you into a fuller awareness of the challenge itself and your emotional reaction to it.

LOOK TO YOUR SELF FOR THE SOLUTION

Others can help you arrive at your own understanding, but no one ever solves your problems for you. Even in circumstances where someone else is acting as an authority or partner, only you can decide for yourself how you will process the situation. The longer you spend searching for guidance outside of yourself, the longer you spend ignoring the problem. Even those who appear to help are only acting as instruments in the greater process of love and grace that is the true nature of your relationship to the universe.

Stop looking for the easy way out or the wise words that will show you the way. Assess the situation, your resources, and your abilities, and then act. Your action may include enlisting help from others, but it will be your challenge to solve. The sooner you take up the challenge, the quicker it stops being a problem.

KNOW YOURSELF

There is a reason why certain challenges seem hard to you while others breeze right through the same situations. There is a reason why you put off a task for weeks that can be done several times a day by someone else. It is not because they have anything over you or are better than you. And it has nothing to do with a particular skill set or know-how. It is all about consciousness. Those who face challenging tasks have found a way to avoid seeing those activities as challenges. Challenges are opportunities to grow. That growth takes place out of potentiality, your potentiality, which is infinite and highly active in every moment of life. Come to know yourself like that. You are pure potential experiencing life through what seems like a limitation. Challenges are spikes in that imaginary limitation barrier that guide you to awareness.

You decide: Are you limited or are you an ever-expansive growth of consciousness and love? Choose the latter, and taking another look at that so-called challenge you have been facing. With your potential, you can turn a mountain of a challenge into a speck of dust, take that dreaded project and turn it into that thing you did before lunch today.

DETACH FROM THE OUTCOME

Stressing about the potential outcome is often what turns a molehill into a mountain. Once you shift your focus to the thing you are actually doing, instead of the result, the most intimidating parts of the trial start to disappear.

When you attach emotions to the problem, it has power over you. If you simply perform the task at hand without worrying about the outcome, you have power over the situation. Some challenges seem enormous and harsh, but if you remain centered and full of awareness, no challenge is too big to meet with power and grace.